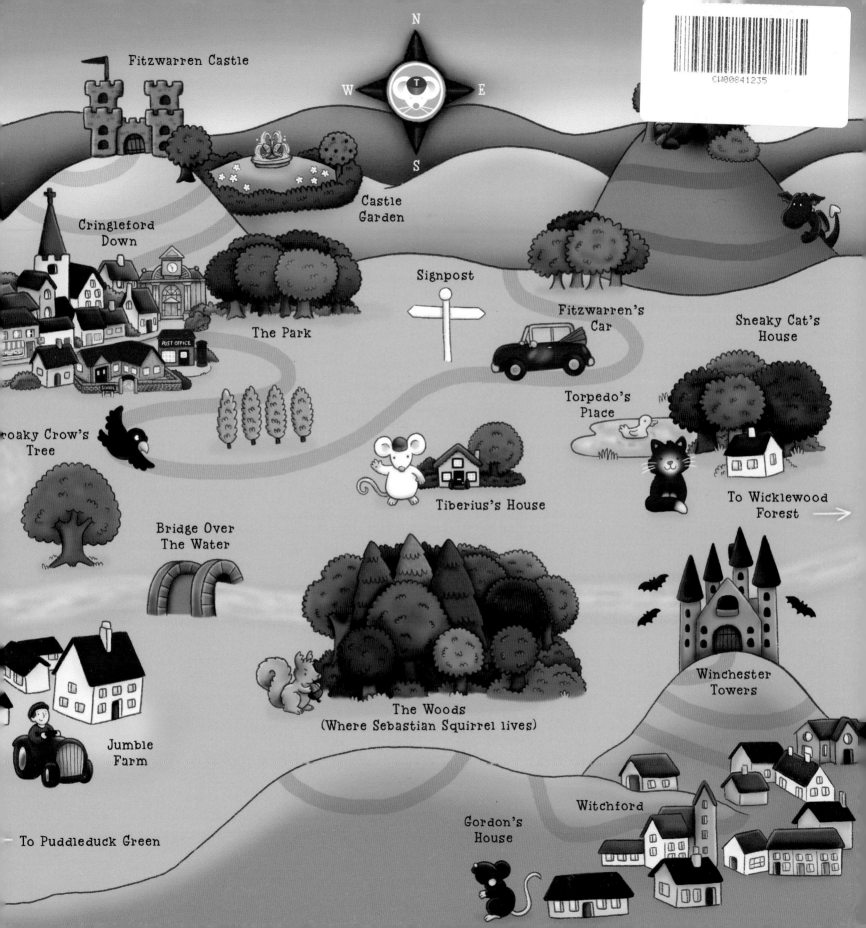

Fitzwarren Castle

N

W E

S

Castle
Garden

Cringleford
Down

The Park

Signpost

Fitzwarren's
Car

Sneaky Cat's
House

Torpedo's
Place

POST OFFICE

SCHOOL

roaky Crow's
Tree

Tiberius's House

To Wicklewood
Forest

Bridge Over
The Water

The Woods
(Where Sebastian Squirrel lives)

Winchester
Towers

Jumble
Farm

Witchford

To Puddleduck Green

Gordon's
House

First published by Tiberius Publishing Ltd

Tiberius Publishing at Orchard Toys
Wymondham Business Park
Wymondham
Norfolk
NR18 9SB

Written by Keith Harvey
Illustrated by Paula Hickman

ISBN 978-1-902604-23-7

Printed in the U.K.

Tiberius
goes
Camping

Written by Keith Harvey
Illustrated by Paula Hickman

 Tiberius Publishing Ltd

Tiberius, Sneaky Cat, Croaky Crow and
Drag the Dragon planned to go
camping at Wicklewood Forest.
There was just one problem;
they didn't have a tent big
enough for Drag!

"What are we going to do?" asked Sneaky.
Tiberius scratched his head. He was thinking.
"I know," he said, with a big smile. "We will make one!"
Tiberius fetched some tarpaulin from his garage and
after much cutting and stitching they had made a tent

Drag put up the homemade
tent in the garden. It had a zip at one end to make an entrance
and tree branches for poles. Drag was really pleased. He was ready
to go with his friends on their camping trip.

When they arrived at Wicklewood Forest, Tiberius and
Sneaky Cat set up their tent close to the river.
Drag said he would prefer to be by the woods
away from the noise of the running water.
They had a lovely day playing games
and cooking their meals in the open air.
"This is so exciting," said Drag, "but the
fresh air has made me feel very tired."
His three friends laughed at him.
"Oh you are always sleepy,"
said Croaky.

Croaky was sharing Drag's tent.
"I might wake you up if I go to bed later,
so I'll come too."
They both said good night to Sneaky and Tiberius.
Before long Sneaky and Tiberius crept into
their own tent and snuggled down for the night.
"Isn't this wonderful," said Tiberius to Sneaky,
"listening to all the noises of the night. The
rustling of the leaves in the trees, the rush of water
in the river and the sound of an owl hooting."
"Absolutely wonderful," said Sneaky sleepily as
they both drifted off to sleep.

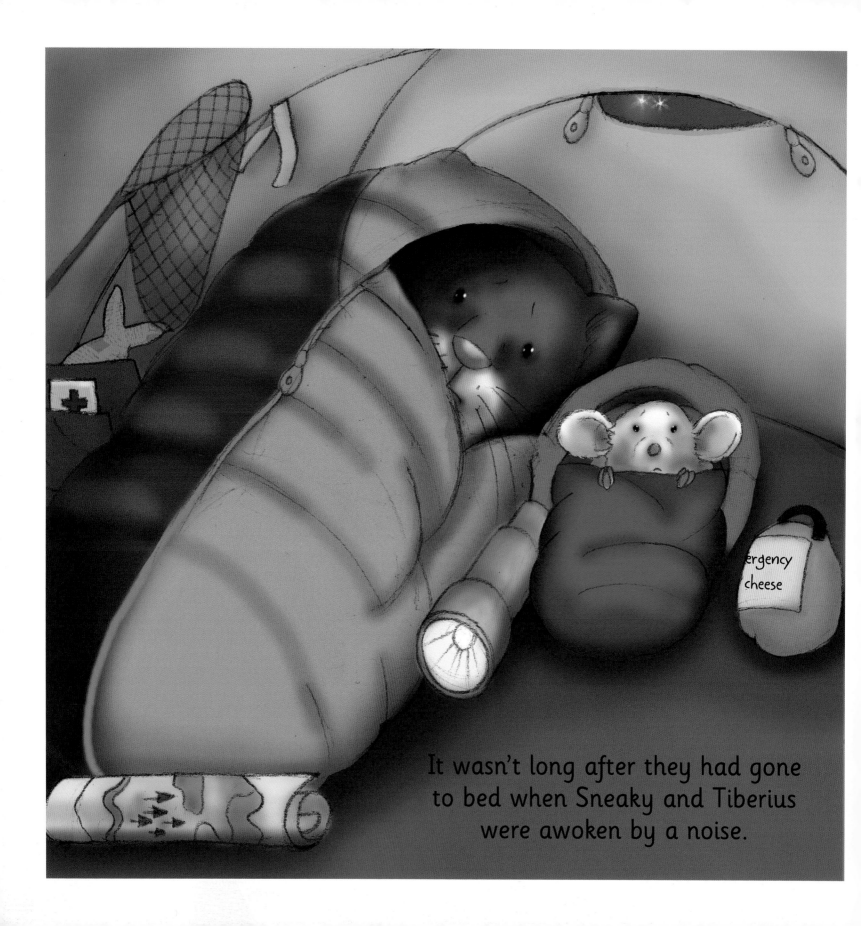

It wasn't long after they had gone
to bed when Sneaky and Tiberius
were awoken by a noise.

"Are you
awake Tiberius?"
whispered Sneaky.
"Of course I am," said Tiberius.
"I can't sleep with all that noise!"
It was a loud thundering, grumbling,
rumbling sound. As they listened, it
became louder and louder and after each
rumble there was a high pitched screech.

GRUMBLE, RUMBLE, SCREECH, SCREECH!!

Sneaky was becoming quite scared.
"What on earth is that?" he asked.
"I've no idea," said Tiberius, who was also rather
worried. "Perhaps we should investigate?"
They peeked out of the tent but could not see anything.
Sneaky picked up a torch and followed his brave
friend out of the tent.

Sneaky's paws trembled as he tried to hold the torch steady.
"Shh, did you hear that noise again?" he said.

Grrrrrummmble
Rummmmble
screech
screech!!

Was it a storm brewing or was it some fearsome creature on the way to the camp? "We should warn Drag and Croaky," said Tiberius, "but shall we explore first?"

They crept in and out
between the trees.
The wind whistled through
the leaves making it very eerie.
Tiberius and Sneaky came
across the owl in a tree
whom they had heard hooting.
He was quiet now, sitting on a
branch with his eyes wide open.
Owls are very wise,
so Tiberius asked if he
knew where the scary
noise was coming from.
"Nooo, Nooo, I don't.
In fact I'm quite worried,"
replied the owl.
"So are we," said Tiberius.
"We are just trying to
find out where and what it is."
"May I come with you?"
asked the owl.
"Of course," replied Tiberius.
The three of them set
off in search of the
mysterious noise.

They hadn't gone much further when they met a fox hiding behind a tree.
"What's that awful sound?" said the fox to the three brave investigators.
"We don't know, we are trying to find out."

GRUMBLE, RUMBLE, SCREECH, SCREECH!!
"I don't like being here on my own, can I come with you?" said the fox.
"Of course," said Tiberius. "The more of us there are, the safer we'll be."

Grrrrrummmble
Rummmble

It wasn't long before they met a goose, who would
usually make an awful noise if there were strangers about.
The goose was sitting very quietly looking around.
"Where are you all going?" she asked.

screech
screech!

"We are looking for that strange noise that you can hear.
Would you like to come with us?" asked Tiberius.
"Oh yes please," said the goose. "I don't want to be left on my own."

They walked past a rabbit burrow. A rabbit popped her head out.
She looked at Tiberius and his companions.
"This noise is keeping all my children awake. Where is it coming from?"
"We are on our way to find out," explained Tiberius.
"May I come with you?" asked the rabbit.
"Of course," said Tiberius.

Tiberius looked at his motley crew. "Before we go any further," he said,
"we should fetch Drag and Croaky to help us in our search."
So off they went: the fox, the owl, the rabbit, the goose,
Sneaky Cat and Tiberius to find Drag and Croaky's tent.
They could still hear the noise.

The noise was growing louder and louder.
They were all feeling very scared. Tiberius knew he would have to be
very brave. He waved one arm and said,
"Follow me. Once Drag is with us we will have nothing to fear."
What his friends didn't see was that Tiberius had
his fingers crossed behind his back.

Grrrrummmble
Rummmble
screech
screech!!

As they approached Drag and Croaky's tent,
Tiberius and Sneaky Cat started giggling.
"This is not a laughing matter," said the owl seriously,
looking down his beak at Tiberius.
"Oh yes it is," laughed Tiberius. "Just you wait and see."

Sneaky Cat peered into Drag's tent.
He shone the torch around the tent.
Croaky was tucked up in his sleeping bag fast asleep.
He was not snoring, but half whistling and half squeaking.

Sneaky shone the torch onto Drag.
Drag was lying on his back snoring so loudly that
the tent poles were shaking!
This was the mysterious noise they had all heard.

Everyone crowded
into Drag's big tent.
Drag suddenly
opened one eye.
"Goodness," he said,
sitting up in bed.
"What are you
all doing here?"

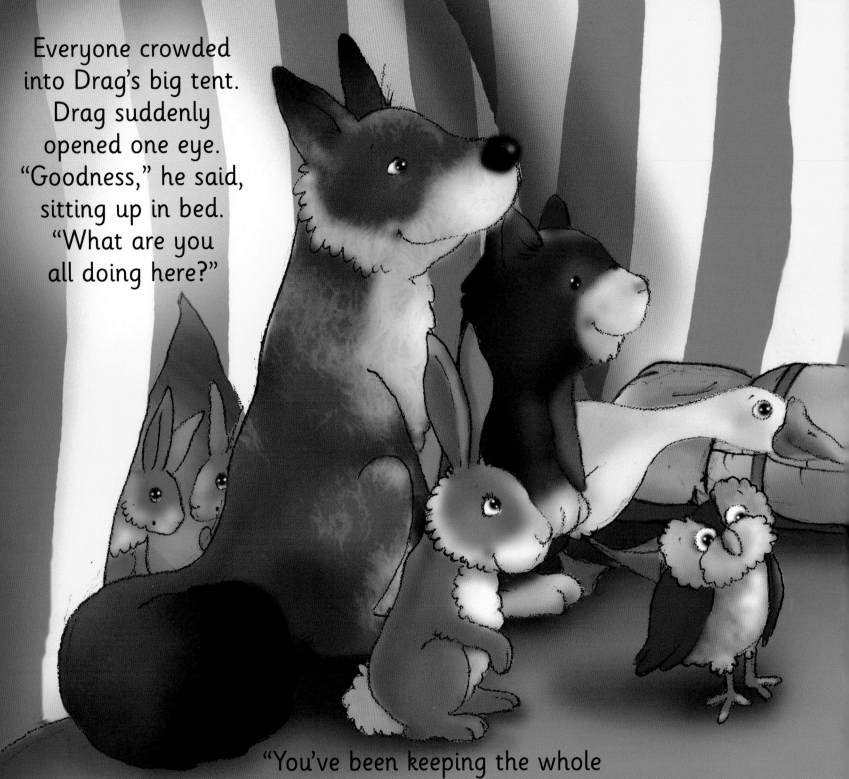

"You've been keeping the whole
campsite awake with your snoring," said Tiberius with a smile.
"Oh no," said Drag, "I'm sorry. I forgot to warn you about my snoring.
When I'm at home in my cave, of course nobody can hear me."

They all breathed
a sigh of relief and
turned to leave.
"Don't go," said Drag
as the clock in the
nearby village struck
12 o'clock.

"I was hoping to have a midnight feast while we were camping,
so shall we have it now with all your new found friends?"
Drag brought out a rucksack from the back of the tent.
You wouldn't believe what was in it!

It was two o'clock in the morning when they had finished eating.
They all said it was the best midnight feast ever.
"Drag," said the owl, looking down his beak,
"that was so good, you must come again!
BUT PROMISE NOT TO SNORE SO LOUDLY."